For my children
Liam Hutchins, Molly Elizabeth, and Kira Rose—
to where you've been and where you're going.
—C.L.

For Jacques, again, who wants to see the world.
—K.K.

Text copyright © 2000 by Christine Loomis. Illustrations copyright © 2000 by Kate Kiesler.

First Edition
1 3 5 7 9 10 8 6 4 2
Printed in Hong Kong by South China Printing Company, Ltd.

This book is set in Bernhard Modern 16/22. The paintings were done in oil paint on bristol board.

Library of Congress Cataloging-in-Publication Data
Loomis, Christine
Across America, I love you / Christine Loomis; illustrated by Kate Kiesler — 1st ed.
p. cm.
Summary: Describes the various landscapes of America, from the Rocky Mountains and Alaska's wild lands to the giant sequoias of California, relating the parent-child relationship to these natural settings.
ISBN 0-7868-0366-5 (trade). — ISBN 0-7868-2314-3 (lib. bdg.)
[1.Parent and child—Fiction. 2. United States—Fiction. 3. Natural history—United States—Fiction.] I. Kiesler, Kate, ill. II. Title.
PZ7.L874Ag 2000
[E]—dc21   99-39075
CIP

Visit www.hyperionchildrensbooks.com, a part of the Network

Across AMERICA, I Love You

I Love You

Written by Christine Loomis & Illustrated by Kate Kiesler

HYPERION BOOKS FOR CHILDREN
New York

Wherever we journey,
Wherever we call home
One thing is always true:
You are part of me
And I am part of you.

In the forests of northern California
branches of giant sequoias
reach up to rock the moon
  and cradle the Western sky,
reach up to embrace a universe of possibilities.
My arms reach, too, ready to rock and cradle you,
to embrace the universe of possibilities in you.

Circling above Alaska's wildlands, unseen,
a mother eagle watches and waits,
waits and watches for her little eagle
to grow into its courage and live its eagle dreams.
With more faith than experience,
    the eaglet must step into thin air and soar.
You will fly to your dreams one day,
and I will sing you on your way.

There are craggy coves and quiet inlets
up and down the rugged Pacific coast,
places where travelers can pause awhile and rest.
It is here that marine animals and seabirds come
when they tire of the freewheeling ocean,
or when storms rage.
I am a cove, an inlet apart from the storms,
a shelter when you wish to come home.

See the Rocky Mountains rise
from the backbone of the continent?
They've stood just so,
    for as long as anyone can remember.
Yet in mountain years they are young
    and still changing.
You are changing, too. Sometimes I can see it,
and sometimes you change like the mountains—
in ways invisible to my eye.
I love who you are and who you will become.

The deserts of America's Southwest—
immense stretches of sand and sage,
   red rock canyons and prickly stands of cactus—
    have a secret.
Each year sudden springs and flowers
   that but briefly bloom transform them into gardens.
You will surprise me when you bloom all at once
   and with little warning.
I will celebrate your surprises.

Watch how the sweet grasses of the prairie
bend with the wind, bowing to a greater force.
But which is stronger?
The winds that blow and howl
or the grasses that so graciously bow?
Sometimes you must bend
and sometimes you must stand against the wind.
It won't always be easy to decide.

It is from the carefully tilled and tended fields
in the heart of the land that nourishment comes.
   Yours and mine.
Squares and circles, rectangles and borders
   etched in earth,
form a living patchwork of plenty.
I nourish you now, though soon you will
learn to feed body and soul on your own.
But in times of wanting,
   there's a place for you at my table.

At its destiny, at the Gulf of Mexico,
   the Mississippi is formidable,
wide and powerful with no need to hurry.
Yet where it begins in Minnesota,
   it's a tiny, rushing stream.
Like the little Mississippi you are young
and rushing toward a destiny that is all your own.
What that is I do not know,
   but if you should need me,
I am here, where you began.

In the damp Southeast are places of mysterious
    beauty,
sanctuaries for the delicate heron
    and deadly alligator alike.
Okefenokee and the Everglades—
    pockets of Mother Earth's deep dreaming
even as civilization strains to swallow them whole.
You must find a sanctuary, too;
    a place within you that is serene and still.
I can't lead you there, but if you listen
    to your heart
and hold fast to your dreams, you will find it.

Do you know that the forests of New England
   play dress-up every fall,
trying on leaves of red and yellow and gold?
However old the forests grow, they still play,
hurling swirling arcs of color
   against the autumn sky.
However old you become, keep playing.
Doing so will neither hasten winter
   nor prevent it from coming.
But a life without laughter is no life at all.

Across the North country crested drifts of snow
fill the forests, bending boughs
    and shaping the land anew.
The wolf, the deer, and the child shiver,
wondering at cold holding spring so deep
    in its soul.
In sunlight, in moonlight,
    in the air, on the trees, on the land
there is white as far as the eye can see
    and still farther.
Yet in all that snowy expanse
not one delicate flake is the same as any other.
You are the only one of you, too—
    a one-of-a-kind child, unique in all the world.

Across America, I love you.

Wherever we journey,
Wherever we call home
One thing is always true:
You are part of me
And I am part of you.